MR. BADGER AND MRS. FOX

THE WILD CAT

Brigitte LUCIANI & Eve THARLET

Graphic Universe™ • Minneapolis

RECEIVED
DEC - - 2018
BY:_____

Story by Brigitte Luciani
Art by Eve Tharlet
Translation by Nathan Sacks

First American edition published in 2018 by Graphic Universe™.
Published by arrangement with MEDIATOON LICENSING—France.

Monsieur Blaireau et Madame Renarde
6/Le Chat Sauvage
© DARGAUD 2016—Tharlet & Luciani
www.dargaud.com

English translation copyright © 2018 by Lerner Publishing Group, Inc.

Graphic Universe™ is a trademark of Lerner Publishing Group, Inc.

All worldwide English-language rights reserved. No part of this book may
be reproduced, stored in a retrieval system, or transmitted in any form
or by any means—electronic, mechanical, photocopying, recording, or otherwise—
without the prior written permission of Lerner Publishing Group, Inc., except
for the inclusion of brief quotations in an acknowledged review.

Graphic Universe™
A division of Lerner Publishing Group, Inc.
241 First Avenue North
Minneapolis, MN 55401 USA

For reading levels and more information, look up this title at www.lernerbooks.com.

Library of Congress Cataloging-in-Publication Data

Names: Luciani, Brigitte, author. | Tharlet, Eve, illustrator. | Sacks, Nathan, translator.
Title: The wild cat / Brigitte Luciani & Eve Tharlet ; translation by Nathan Sacks.
Other titles: Chat sauvage. English
Description: First American edition. | Minneapolis : Graphic Universe, 2018. | Series: Mr.
Badger and Mrs. Fox ; #6 | Originally published in France by Dargaud in 2016 under title: Le
chat sauvage. | Summary: After watching a performance of a wild cat climbing trees, Ginger
the fox decides to learn to climb trees herself, but when she is criticized for not behaving
like a fox, she leaves her blended family behind in search of other foxes. | Identifiers:
LCCN 2017044305 (print) | LCCN 2017058394 (ebook) | ISBN 9781541500884 (eb pdf) |
ISBN 9781541500860 (lb : alk. paper) | ISBN 9781541500877 (pb : alk. paper)
Subjects: LCSH: Graphic novels. | CYAC: Graphic novels. | Self-acceptance—Fiction. |
Stepfamilies—Fiction. | Foxes—Fiction. | Badgers—Fiction.
Classification: LCC PZ7.7.L83 (ebook) | LCC PZ7.7.L83 Wi 2018 (print) | DDC 741.5/973—dc23

LC record available at https://lccn.loc.gov/2017044305

Manufactured in the United States of America
1-43757-33617-3/9/2018

3

Hello! We have a question...

Us too! Who are you?

You may call us the Fabulous Genettes.

Gennifer...

Gena...

And Genevieve.

We're looking for a place to put on a show for tonight.

What show?

A show for the Great Sylvester! The WILD CAT!

HERE?

Yeah!!

Cool!

You can set up in the clearing. We'll show you.

I've never heard of this Sylvester.

He's great—you'll see!

But what's the difference between a normal cat and a wild cat?

They're not AT ALL the same!

But they look the same.

Not even! A wild cat is much stronger.

And bigger.

And flashy!

Pfft.

Also, you can tell a wild cat by the rings on his tail.

HEY! You heard?

Sylvester's doing two shows, one today and one tomorrow.

We're seeing him tonight. How about you?

Us too!

Come on, we'll tell our folks!

What about our game? It's not done yet.

We haven't figured out who Grub was!

We'll finish another time.

Ladybug.

Huh?!

You did it! Berry, you just won! How did you figure out who I am?

Ladybug!

Ooooh!

Aaaaaah!

Sylvesterrr!

An autograph? Please?

Clear the way!

We're gonna try to meet him!

Okay. We're going home with Berry—there are too many fans!

See ya later!

9

That cat has class.

When I grow up, I want to be like him!

Sure, Ginger. There's just one problem. You don't know how to climb trees!

Says who? I've never tried.

Me neither.

Hee hee, I think I know why!

Ginger!

11

You know what I think about little foxes who go climbing up trees?

 I think it's RIDICULOUS.

 Reee-diculous!

 That's Ginger, the daughter of your friend Mr. Fox.

Oh, really? So Basil's little girl thinks she's a squirrel. How delightful.

Ha!

Ha!

Ha!

 What are you doing with those badgers?

I live with them.

 Pff! It doesn't matter.

I pity your father.

 He must be ashamed of you!

Ginger!
Come down!

Bottom first!

If you could avoid falling, we'd appreciate it!

Plop!

Thanks!

You met Sylvester up there!

What did he say?

Drop it! I'm tired. I'm going home.

?!

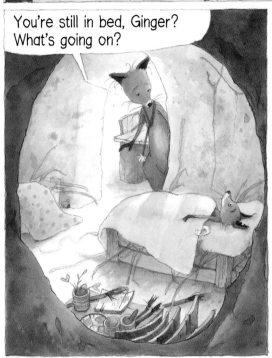

You're still in bed, Ginger? What's going on?

When will Papa come see me?

I'm not sure. You know him. He never tells us first.

Do you think he's angry with me?

Of course not! Why do you ask?

It's been a long time since he visited...

I know...but I'm sure he'll come soon.

He never goes too long without visiting.

And now, HOP UP! The others are already out playing!

We have a visitor, Ma!

Oh, and who's this charming young fox?

My name's Ginger.

Welcome to our foxhole, Ginger!

Not from around here?

Are you lost?

Hello.

You must be tired. Sit down!

Why do you have a split ear?

It looks nice with your white hair!

Where are you from?

Who are you?

Have some locusts, Ginger.

They're good, right?

Mmm!

Let's take a deep breath, everybody.

Pa!

Meanwhile...

I wonder where she went.

There's the Genettes. They might know something.

Hello! Have you seen Ginger?

Who's that again?

The little fox who lives with them.

Oh, that one. She's more **BADGER** than fox!

Ha! Ha! Ha! Ha! Ha! Ha!

Have you seen Ginger— **YES** or **NO**?

Yeah, we saw her.

We saw her running.

Where?

Far.

Far from badgers!

Ha! Ha! Ha!

Grrgh!

Ha ha ha! A badger trying to catch a genet.

How ridiculous!

As ridiculous as a fox who tries to climb trees.

Ha! Ha! Ha!

Hey! Ginger succeeded! She climbed a tree!

What bullies!

I despise them!

Why does Sylvester hang out with them?

We have to teach them a lesson.

But they're too fast for us!

Don't worry. I have an idea.

Want to help?

My pleasure!

Papa!

Looks like she knows him.

Yep! "Mission: Save the Girl" accomplished.

You made some fox friends?

Eighteen of them! And I have lots of other things to tell you.

You see?

Clever!

You are your father's daughter.

Why do you say that? Did you climb trees too?

Sometimes.

Basil! To what do I owe the honor of this visit?

You owe us an explanation, Sylvester.

I hear you think it's ridiculous when a fox climbs trees?

But it was you, years ago, who taught me how to climb!

That's true.

It was a long time ago.

Sure. Back then, you were not quite **THE GREAT WILD CAT.**

Hush! Not so loud.

Come this way. We can speak in private.

Now!

27

28

Forgive me, Ginger! I wasn't nice to you yesterday.

It's not you who's ridiculous.

It's ME.

You try new things. That's brave.

Me, I pretend to be someone I'm not. I'm a coward.

But why don't you say you're a regular cat?

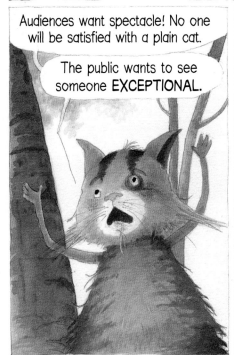

Audiences want spectacle! No one will be satisfied with a plain cat.

The public wants to see someone EXCEPTIONAL.

Anyway, I hate cats...

His parents left him in the forest. He grew up alone.

Poor guy!